Kids Living Green

Let's Eat Green!

by Jenna Lee Gleisner

Bullfrog Books

Ideas for Parents and Teachers

Bullfrog Books let children practice reading informational text at the earliest reading levels. Repetition, familiar words, and photo labels support early readers.

Before Reading
- Discuss the cover photo. What does it tell them?
- Look at the picture glossary together. Read and discuss the words.

Read the Book
- "Walk" through the book and look at the photos. Let the child ask questions. Point out the photo labels.
- Read the book to the child, or have him or her read independently.

After Reading
- Prompt the child to think more. Ask: There are ideas for eating green in this book. What other ways can you think of?

Bullfrog Books are published by Jump!
5357 Penn Avenue South
Minneapolis, MN 55419
www.jumplibrary.com

Copyright © 2019 Jump! International copyright reserved in all countries. No part of this book may be reproduced in any form without written permission from the publisher.

Library of Congress Cataloging-in-Publication Data is available at www.loc.gov or upon request from the publisher.

ISBN: 978-1-64128-450-9 (hardcover)
ISBN: 978-1-64128-451-6 (paperback)
ISBN: 978-1-64128-452-3 (ebook)

Editor: Susanne Bushman
Designer: Molly Ballanger

Photo Credits: Steve Debenport/iStock, cover; Santhosh Varghese/Shutterstock, 1; KK Tan/Shutterstock, 3; Fertnig/iStock, 4 (foreground); BLUR LIFE 1975/Shutterstock, 4 (background); graletta/Shutterstock, 5; nuttapong/iStock, 6–7, 23tl, 23bl; GlobalStock/iStock, 8; Elenathewise/iStock, 9; Hill Street Studios/Superstock, 10–11; xavierarnau/iStock, 12–13, 23tr; Rawpixel.com/Shutterstock, 13; Africa Studio/Shutterstock, 14; Dorling Kindersley: Dave King/Getty, 15; Cultura Limited/Superstock, 16–17; monkeybusinessimages/iStock, 18–19; Wavebreakmedia/iStock, 20–21; JeniFoto/Shutterstock, 22 (blueberries), 22 (raspberries); Danny Smythe/Shutterstock, 22 (potatoes); Volkova Vera/Shutterstock, 23br; Sarah Noda/Shutterstock, 24.

Printed in the United States of America at Corporate Graphics in North Mankato, Minnesota.

Table of Contents

Eat Green	4
Let's Do It!	22
Picture Glossary	23
Index	24
To Learn More	24

Eat Green

Sam eats green.

What does this mean?
He makes healthy choices.

Eating green means more.

Delivering food is bad for Earth.

It pollutes.

How can we help?

Lou grows a garden!

The food is in his yard!

garden bed

Hank and Liz have chickens.

They share the eggs.

Mel shops near her house.

Where?

The farmer's market!

Rita clears her plate. She does not waste.

She makes frozen treats with fruit.

Why?

To use fruit before it spoils.

Ben eats fresh oranges.

Tia and Finn make their own pizzas.

Nice!

You can eat green every day.

How will you do it?

Let's Do It!

Eat Local

Part of eating green is eating local. What does this mean? Eating the fresh foods grown around us. They don't have to be delivered.

You can eat local many ways. Grow your own food in a garden. Or a community garden. Shop at a farmer's market. Eat food that is in season. Freeze food that is in season so you can eat it when it's not growing.

Find food that grows near you. Have an adult help you find a recipe with those foods. You can make them together at home! This is eating green!

Picture Glossary

delivering
Using transportation to take or send something to a person or place.

farmer's market
A food market at which local farmers sell their fresh fruits and vegetables directly to buyers.

pollutes
Makes dirty or impure, especially with waste or other products produced by humans.

spoils
Becomes rotten or unfit for eating.

Index

chickens 10
delivering 7
eggs 10
farmer's market 13
fruit 15
garden 8
healthy 5
oranges 17
pizzas 18
pollutes 7
spoils 15
waste 14

To Learn More

Finding more information is as easy as 1, 2, 3.
❶ Go to www.factsurfer.com
❷ Enter "let'seatgreen!" into the search box.
❸ Click the "Surf" button to see a list of websites.